DINOFOURS™
I'M THE BOSS!

For Uncle Bill
— S.M.

Text copyright © 1998 by Scholastic Inc.
Illustrations copyright © 1998 by Hans Wilhelm, Inc.
All rights reserved. Published by Scholastic Inc.
CARTWHEEL BOOKS and the CARTWHEEL BOOKS logo
are trademarks and/or registered trademarks of Scholastic Inc.

Library of Congress Cataloging-in-Publication Data

Metzger, Steve.
    I'm the boss! / by Steve Metzger; illustrated by Hans Wilhelm.
      p.   cm. — (Dinofours)
    "Cartwheel books."
    Summary: Tara learns a lesson about being too bossy when everyone leaves the game after she wants everything her way.
    ISBN 0-590-37458-3
    [1. Behavior—Fiction.   2. Nursery schools—Fiction.   3. Schools—Fiction.
  4. Dinosaurs—Fiction.]
    I. Wilhelm, Hans, 1945-   ill.   II. Title.   III. Series: Metzger, Steve. Dinofours.
    PZ7.M56775Im   1998
    [E]—dc21   97-7315
                                                   CIP
                                                   AC

10 9 8 7 6 5 4 3 2   8 9/9 0/0 01 02

Printed in the U.S.A.   24
First printing, March 1998

DINOFOURS™

I'M THE BOSS!

by Steve Metzger
Illustrated by Hans Wilhelm

Cartwheel
·B·O·O·K·S·®

SCHOLASTIC INC.
New York Toronto London Auckland Sydney

Mrs. Dee had just finished reading *Goldilocks and the Three Bears*. Now it was time to go outside.

As the children lined up by the door, Tara said, "I love that story. Let's play *Goldilocks and the Three Bears* in the playground. Who wants to play with me?"

"I do," said Joshua.

"Me, too," said Tracy.

Brendan, Danielle, and Albert wanted to play as well.

"Let's play in the big blocks area!" Tara shouted as they walked outside.

The children followed Tara.
"Before we start, I have something
to tell you," she said. Then Tara sang:

I'm the boss.
This is my game.
Listen to me now!
I will tell you what to do,
and I will tell you how!

"I'm leaving," said Joshua. "This doesn't sound like a fun game to me."

"That's okay," Tara said cheerfully. "We still have lots of people who want to play."

Tara stood on one of the tree stumps.
"I'm going to be Goldilocks," she announced.
"But I want to be Goldilocks," Tracy said.
"No," said Tara. "I'm the boss, so I'm Goldilocks."

"Mrs. Dee! Mrs. Dee!" shouted Tracy. "Tara is being too bossy. I want to be Goldilocks, but she won't let me."

"It's my game and I'm Goldilocks," Tara said.

"Why don't both of you play the part of Goldilocks?" Mrs. Dee suggested. "You can take turns."

Tracy nodded yes.

"That's a bad idea," said Tara. "There's only one Goldilocks and that's me."

"No fair!" said Tracy as she stomped away. "I'm not playing!"

"Well, Tara," said Mrs. Dee, "this game might be more fun for your friends if you listened to their ideas, too."

"I won't!" said Tara. "I'm the boss and that's that!"

"All right," said Mrs. Dee. "Let's see what happens."

Mrs. Dee walked to the nearby climber.

"I'll be over here if you need me," she said.

Tara turned to face the other children.

"Danielle," she said, "you're Mama Bear because you're a girl. Albert, you're Papa Bear. And, Brendan, you're Baby Bear."

"Why?" asked Brendan.

"Because sometimes you act like a baby," Tara replied.

"I do not act like a baby!" Brendan yelled. "I should be the Papa Bear because I'm big and I have a loud voice."

Brendan stood up tall.

"Someone's been sleeping in my bed!" he shouted.

"I'm sorry," said Tara. "But I'm the boss and you're Baby Bear."

"No, I'm not," said Brendan, walking away.

Tara, Danielle, and Albert were the only children left.

"What are we going to do now?" asked Albert. "There's only enough of us for Goldilocks and two bears."

"That's okay," said Tara. "I'll be Goldilocks *and* Baby Bear! Now let's begin. Pretend we're in the three bears' house in the forest."

Tara began to stack some blocks.

"Help me make the table where Mama Bear, Papa Bear, and Baby Bear are eating their porridge," she said.

Danielle and Albert helped Tara build the table. When they finished, Tara turned to Danielle.

"Bring me three containers from the sandbox," Tara ordered. "We need them for our porridge bowls."

"You didn't ask me in a nice way," said Danielle. "My mommy says you should always say, 'Please.'"

"I'm the boss," said Tara. "I don't have to say, 'Please.'"

"I don't like this game anymore," said Danielle, leaving the blocks area. "I'm going to play with Tracy."

"I'll get the bowls myself," said Tara, walking to the sandbox.

When she came back, the only child left was Albert.

"All right," said Tara. "I'll be Goldilocks, Baby Bear, *and* Mama Bear."

"Okay," said Albert.

"Let's build two chairs," said Tara.

Tara and Albert made chairs by stacking two square blocks. They sat down.

"Albert, make believe you're eating porridge and it's too hot."

Albert pretended to eat the porridge from his bowl.

"Ow!" Albert exclaimed in a deep, Papa Bear voice. "My porridge is much too hot!"

"Now, I'll be Mama Bear and Baby Bear and pretend my porridge is too hot, too," said Tara.

"It's too hot!" she said, tasting her porridge, first as Mama Bear, then as Baby Bear.

Tara quickly stood up.

"Now, let's go for a walk, Papa Bear," Tara said in her best Mama Bear voice.

"Okay," said Albert as Papa Bear. Then he said, "Someone's been eating my porridge."

"No! No!" said Tara. "You're not supposed to say that now. Goldilocks hasn't even been here yet."

Then she shouted, "You don't know how to play!"

"I don't care," said Albert, walking away. "Good-bye!"

Mrs. Dee walked over and sat down.

"It's no fun playing *Goldilocks and the Three Bears* by myself," Tara said to Mrs. Dee.

"I'm sorry the other children left your game," Mrs. Dee said. "Why do you think that happened?"

"I don't know," said Tara. "Maybe I was a little too bossy."

"Perhaps you were," said Mrs. Dee. "Tara, how do you feel when people are bossy with you?"

"I don't like it!" said Tara.

"That's probably a good thing to remember when you play with your friends," Mrs. Dee said.

"Okay," Tara said, "I'll try."

"Tara, you have such wonderful ideas," Mrs. Dee said. "When we go outside tomorrow, I'm sure your friends will want to play with you again."

"Maybe they won't," said Tara. "And I want to play *The Three Little Pigs and the Big Bad Wolf*. That's a fun game."

"Do you want to ask them?" asked Mrs. Dee.

Tara nodded.

Mrs. Dee called the children over to the big blocks area.

"Tara has something to ask you," Mrs. Dee said.

"When we go outside tomorrow," said Tara, "I want to play *The Three Little Pigs and the Big Bad Wolf*. Does anyone want to play? I won't be so bossy."

"I do," said Danielle.

"I want to be the Big Bad Wolf," Tracy called out.

"But I wanted to be . . . ," Tara said.

Remembering what she had just said to Mrs. Dee, Tara stopped and thought.

"Okay, Tracy," Tara said. "You can be the Big Bad Wolf. I'll be one of the pigs."

Now the other children wanted to play, too.

"I'm sure tomorrow's game will be much better than today's," Mrs. Dee said.

Then, Tara sang a new song:

Today I was too bossy.
It had to be my way.
Tomorrow will be different,
When we go out to play.

It was time to put away the blocks and go inside.